Gabriella

the
Snow Kingdom
Fairy

For Alex Goodfellow, with lots of love
Special thanks to Sue Mongredien

No part of this work may be reproduced, stored in a retrieval system, or transmitted in any form or by any means, electronic, mechanical, photocopying, recording, or otherwise, without written permission of the publisher. For information regarding permission, write to Rainbow Magic Limited, c/o HIT Entertainment, 830 South Greenville Avenue, Allen, TX 75002-3320.

ISBN 978-0-545-62765-8

10 9 8 7 6 5 4 3 2   14 15 16 17 18/0
Printed in the U.S.A.   40

First printing, September 2009

Gabriella

the
Snow Kingdom
Fairy

by Daisy Meadows

SCHOLASTIC INC.

New York   Toronto   London   Auckland
Sydney   Mexico City   New Delhi   Hong Kong

Jack Frost's
Ice Castle

Mountains

Ski Slopes

Toasted
Bogmallows
← Stall

Bonfire

Ice Sculptures

Gabriella's Magic
Snowflake

It's icy cold and freezing, now that winter's here.
Snowstorms, ice, and sleet – my favorite time of year.
But what's this – smiling faces? People having fun?
I think I'll try to spoil the snow for everyone!

The magic snowflake I will steal;
the silver chest and firestone, too.
How they'll shiver, how they'll sigh,
when my work is through!

**Find the hidden letters in the snowballs
throughout this book. Unscramble all 6 letters to
make a special winter word!**

Contents

A Fairy Snowball!

"We're going to try out the slopes,"
Kirsty Tate called to her mom. "We'll be
back for lunch."

"See you later!" Rachel Walker
shouted to her mom and dad.

The two friends grinned at each other
as their parents called back good-byes.
Both girls were wearing new ski outfits,

knitted hats, and gloves. Kirsty pushed
open the door of the ski lodge, and
they stepped out into the bright sunshine.

Mountain peaks rose majestically
all around, covered in thick white
snow. Skiers were already racing down
the slopes in colorful groups. Other
people were careening around on
snowboards, sun glinting off their
snow goggles.

Rachel couldn't stop smiling. "It's so fantastic being on vacation with you again!" she said.

Kirsty nodded. "I know," she agreed, linking arms with her best friend. "All this snow, and the Winter Festival starts in a few days, too!" She beamed. "And you never know, we might meet a fairy. We always have such magical adventures when we're together!"

The girls' parents had rented them each
skis and a snowboard. Rachel and Kirsty
went to find them in the small shed at the
side of the lodge. "I'm going to try my
skis first," Kirsty decided. She grabbed a
pair of ski poles, skis, and special ski
boots, and sat down to put them on.

"I'll try the snowboard," Rachel
said eagerly. She picked up a turquoise
board that was long and slender, with
round ends.

When the girls were both ready,
they found a small slope to
practice on.

"*Wheeee!*" Kirsty squealed,
pushing off. "Here I go!"
She flew down the slope,
but wobbled at the end
and crashed sideways
in the icy snow. She
got to her feet
gingerly and
rubbed her legs.

"My turn
now. . . . Yay!"
cried Rachel,

standing on her board and riding
downhill. It was tricky keeping her
balance, and she tumbled into the snow.
"Ow!" she cried, as her elbow hit a
particularly icy patch. "This snow isn't
very soft, is it?"

Kirsty shook her head. "Look at that girl over there," she whispered, helping her friend up. "The snow's so crumbly, she can't even build her snowman!"

Rachel watched the girl struggle with her snowman nearby. The snow wasn't clumping together. Instead, it fell apart into ice chips.

"Maybe we should leave skiing and snowboarding for later," Rachel suggested. "How about a snowball fight?"

"You're on!" Kirsty laughed as she quickly unstrapped her skis.

The girls started making snowballs, but the snow didn't stick together very well.

And then, when they threw them at each other, the snowballs were so hard that they really hurt!

Rachel had just opened her mouth to suggest they try something else, when she saw a snowball flying toward her face. Before she could duck, the snowball burst apart in a puff of sparkling snow crystals.

Rachel jumped in surprise. Hovering in midair, right where the snowball had been, was a fairy! "Oh!" gasped Rachel. "Hello! Who are you?" The fairy had chestnut-brown hair and fluffy white earmuffs that were shiny with silver glitter. She wore a purple coat with a red-and-purple striped dress

underneath, red leggings, and purple
snow boots.

"I'm Gabriella,"
the fairy said, as she
curtsied. "Gabriella the
Snow Kingdom Fairy.
And I'm really glad
to see you here!"
Kirsty hurried over.
"Hi, Gabriella," she said
to the tiny fairy. "I'm Kirsty.
Is everything all right?"

Gabriella shook her head sadly.
"No," she said. "Jack Frost is up to his
tricks again! He's stolen my special
magic snowflake, which makes all the
snow soft, fluffy, and white. Now that it's
missing, snow everywhere is much harder
and icier."

"We noticed," Kirsty said. "How did he get your snowflake?"

"Well, every year on the first of December, I hang my magic snowflake on the Christmas tree outside the Fairyland palace," Gabriella explained. "But this morning, the snowflake was gone — and there were goblin footprints all around the tree. I'm sure Jack Frost ordered his goblins to steal it and hide it in the human world."

"We'll help you look for it," Rachel said.

"Thank you," Gabriella said gratefully. "I'm afraid it'll be difficult to spot. The only clue

will be a patch of snow that looks perfectly sparkly and fluffy. That could mean my magic snowflake is nearby."

Kirsty gazed around, then frowned as she noticed that it was snowing over a nearby pine forest. "How weird," she commented. "It's snowing there — but not here!" Gabriella swung around to see. She tilted her head as she looked carefully at the falling flakes. A smile appeared on her face. "They look like perfect snowflakes to me," she declared.

"Does that mean . . . ?" Rachel began excitedly.

Gabriella nodded. "I'm sure my magic snowflake must be in that forest. Let's go and look!"

Freeze!

The three friends set off to investigate. They made their way through the pine trees and saw a small clearing ahead. They could hear voices calling out in the crisp morning air, and as they got closer to the clearing, they saw that it was full of goblins!

"Hide!" Kirsty said, darting behind a spiky pine tree. Rachel and Gabriella followed. They couldn't let the goblins spot them — they would guess that the girls and Gabriella were looking for the magic snowflake.

Rachel, Kirsty, and Gabriella peeked cautiously through the branches of the pine tree. The goblins were having a great time playing in the snow . . . and it seemed to be very fluffy snow, too!

"My snowflake *must* be nearby," Gabriella whispered. "That snow looks perfect. So do the falling flakes. They're so fluffy and soft!"

"We'll have to get closer so we can take a better look," Rachel replied. "But it'll be tricky with all those goblins around."

"Don't forget to keep an eye out for interfering fairies," one of the goblins said to his friends just then. "Jack Frost gave me strict instructions not to let any of them near our snowflake!"

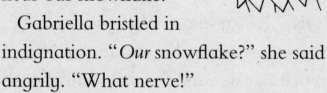

Gabriella bristled in indignation. "*Our* snowflake?" she said angrily. "What nerve!"

"Maybe if we had some kind of disguise, we could sneak up on them," Kirsty suggested. "It would have to be

something white, of course, with all this snow around."

Rachel grinned. "We could be snowmen!" she said. "Gabriella, can you use your magic to make us look like snowmen?"

"Yes, of course — what a great idea!" Gabriella exclaimed. "But snowmen don't usually *walk*, so my magic will only make you look like snowmen when you're very still."

"OK," Kirsty said. "We'll just have to inch forward a tiny bit at a time." She propped her skis and Rachel's snowboard by a tree. "And we'll freeze whenever a goblin looks our way."

"Speaking of freezing . . ." Gabriella waved her wand. A swirl of blue and red fairy dust shaped like tiny snowballs streamed around the girls. Soon they looked like round, white snowmen, complete with hats, scarves, and carrot noses.

"Fantastic!" Rachel laughed, and clapped her hands together. But as she moved, her own arms became visible and the snowman illusion vanished. It was only when she was perfectly still again that her disguise returned.

"This is going to be hard," she said. "But we have to try."

"Good luck!" Gabriella whispered. The girls slowly inched forward. They stopped every time they thought one of the goblins was going to look their way. It was nerve-wracking! Kirsty's heart thumped as she and Rachel

shuffled closer and closer. They were almost close enough to hear the goblins muttering to one another. Only a few more steps, and they'd be able to listen in on everything!

But just then, one of the goblins spun around and saw them. "Hey!" he shouted to his friends. "Look over there!"

A Special Discovery

Rachel and Kirsty were so scared they could barely breathe. Had they been discovered?

"Look at those snowmen!" the goblin said to his friends. "Cool!"

A pointy-nosed goblin stared. "Who built them?" he wondered. "I didn't notice them before." He got up as if he

were about to take a closer look, and
Rachel and Kirsty were both filled with
dread. If he came too close, he'd surely
realize they weren't *real* snowmen!

Luckily, a goblin with big ears pulled
the pointy-nosed goblin back down to
where he'd been sitting on a log.

"There's no more time for playing
around," he said sternly.
"We have to start getting
ready for Jack Frost's
party."

Kirsty and Rachel both held their breath as they listened to the goblins' conversation.

Jack Frost was having a big winter party at his Ice Castle in Fairyland. He wanted the snow around his castle to be perfect so everyone would have fun playing in it. That was why he'd stolen the magic snowflake! "Of course, he's even happier now that the rest of the snow has been ruined for the fairies and the humans!" chortled the big-eared goblin.

Meanwhile, Gabriella had fluttered to hide behind Kirsty so that she could also listen in on the goblins. Kirsty could feel Gabriella's wings quiver with irritation as she heard what the goblins were saying.

Then Rachel spotted something. Two goblins were throwing a white and sparkly object to one another like a Frisbee. "Gabriella!" she hissed. "Is that your snowflake?"

Gabriella peeked over Kirsty's snowman hat. "Yes!" she squeaked. "There it is!"

The snowflake certainly seemed very magical. Whenever one of the goblins missed a catch, the snowflake hit the ground with a huge puff of sparkling white snow. The goblins had to dig it out of a mini-snowdrift each time they dropped it.

Just as the girls were wondering how they would be able to get the snowflake back, the nearest goblin missed his catch again. Gabriella's magic snowflake landed not far from the girls. On impulse,

both Kirsty and Rachel dashed toward it, intending to dig the snowflake out of its snowdrift. But of course, the snowman illusion vanished — the girls were suddenly very visible to the goblins!

Race Down the Mountain

"Hey!" cried a goblin. "Those snowmen just turned into girls!"

Kirsty and Rachel dug frantically in the snow. Where was that snowflake?

"They're trying to steal our magic snowflake!" another goblin realized. "Quick — stop them!"

Immediately, the goblins all
rushed to the snowdrift
and began speedily
scooping away at
the snow. They
were desperate
to get to the
snowflake
before the
girls did.

Rachel and
Kirsty dug
just as quickly,
but snow was now
flying everywhere.
It was getting very
hard to see!

"Got it!" cried a goblin
triumphantly, leaping to his feet

with the sparkly white
magic snowflake
in his hand.
"Run!" another
goblin bellowed.
He kicked a
pile of snow
into the girls'
faces, and
then he
and the other
goblins ran
to grab their
sleds and
snowboards.
Within seconds,
they were all
speeding away
into the distance.

Kirsty and Rachel wiped the snow from their eyes. "Let's grab our skis and snowboard. We can't let them escape!" Kirsty cried.

"Let me help," Gabriella said. She waved her wand and fairy dust spiraled from its tip. The snowboard and skis rose up from where the girls had left them propped against the tree and flew through the air in a cloud of glittering blue sparkles. The snowboard landed right at Rachel's feet. The skis arranged themselves in front of Kirsty and the poles flew into her hands. The

girls' snowmen disguises vanished
for good.

"Thanks, Gabriella," Kirsty said, as she
fastened her skis. "Let's go!"

The goblins were off in the distance by
now, so the girls and Gabriella gave
chase. Fresh snow from the magic
snowflake fell and blurred their view, but
the goblins were yelling and
making so much noise
that they were easy
to track.

The goblins disappeared over the side of a mountain slope, and when Kirsty, Rachel, and Gabriella reached the edge, they saw that the goblins were zooming down at top speed.

Rachel held her breath as she and Kirsty began racing down the slope. She hadn't had much practice on a snowboard, and this was a steep mountain — she really hoped she'd be able to keep her balance. Kirsty also felt

nervous on her skis. She'd only ever tried them out on the bunny slopes before. But both girls knew Gabriella's fairy magic would help them keep up with the goblins — it was their only hope of getting the magic snowflake back!

"You're doing really well," Gabriella called out. "I think we're gaining on them. Keep going!"

It was true. The girls were getting closer and closer to the goblins. Kirsty could see that the goblin with the snowflake wasn't far away, and she hunched a little lower on her skis, trying to catch up with him. Just as she was about to reach him, however, another goblin pulled up alongside them on a snowboard. Deftly, he plucked the snowflake out of the first goblin's hands.

Luckily, Rachel was near the goblin who now had the snowflake. As she zoomed past on her snowboard, she flung out a hand and grabbed the snowflake from the surprised goblin.

Rachel gasped in shock — partly because she'd actually saved Gabriella's

magic snowflake, but also because it was very cold to the touch, even through her gloves! It numbed her fingers, and she couldn't get a good grip on it.

"Oh no!" Rachel cried helplessly, as it fell from her grasp. Her frozen fingers just couldn't hold on anymore. She tried desperately to stop her snowboard, but she was going too fast. Rachel could only turn and watch as the snowflake floated through the air behind her.

A Snowy Surprise

"Ha, ha!" A goblin sliding along on a sled grabbed the magic snowflake and cheered with glee.

Rachel finally managed to stop her snowboard, and Kirsty pulled up beside her.

"Sorry," Rachel groaned, disappointed

with herself. "I wasn't expecting the magic snowflake to be so cold."

"Don't worry," Kirsty said. "I've got an idea. Gabriella, do you think you could use your magic to create a huge snowdrift at the bottom of the mountain? We could catch all the goblins in it!"

"Sure," Gabriella replied. "Let's see . . ." She pointed her wand down and chanted some magic words. Blue and red sparkles crackled from her wand, and an enormous pile of snow appeared at the foot of the mountain. The goblins, who were all careening down the slope, plunged straight into it!

Gabriella giggled. "It's a nice, soft landing for them, at least," she said, as muffled shouts came from the snowdrift. Goblin arms and legs stuck out everywhere, but none of the goblins seemed able to get out.

"Come on," Kirsty said with a grin. "Let's see if we can find the snowflake now that all the goblins are trapped."

She and Rachel went down to the
bottom of the mountain, stopping just
before they reached the goblin snow
heap. "There it is," Rachel said happily.
A green hand poked out from the snow,
its knobbly fingers curled
around the magic
snowflake.

"Hooray!" cried Gabriella, flying over.
She touched the snowflake with her
wand, and it immediately glowed bright
red with fairy magic and shrank down to
its Fairyland size.

The fairy looked delighted. "Thank you, girls," she said. "Now I can put the magic snowflake back where it should be — on the Fairyland Christmas tree. This time, I'll tie it on with some magic tinsel to keep anyone from stealing it!" She kissed Kirsty and Rachel happily. "That way, all the snow in Fairyland and in your world will be perfect — just what you need for winter vacation fun!"

Rachel and Kirsty beamed at the little fairy and said good-bye. With that, Gabriella vanished in a cloud of blue sparkles. The girls turned to see that

the goblins had climbed out of the
snowdrift, and were stomping off with
their heads down.

"That was fun," Rachel said. "I loved racing down the mountain like that."

"Me, too," said Kirsty. "It's turning out to be another fantastic fairy adventure . . . and it's only getting started!"

Contents

Stolen!

The next morning was bright and sunny.
After their exciting adventure the day
before, Kirsty and Rachel couldn't wait
to get back on the slopes.

"The snow looks perfect," Rachel said
happily, as she and Kirsty tramped along.
"Gabriella must have gotten the magic
snowflake back to Fairyland."

"I love the way the snow feels under my boots," Kirsty said. "It's so deep and soft — just right."

Rachel gazed around, appreciating the glittering white blanket of snow that covered everything. But then she noticed something strange. "Nobody seems very happy," she murmured to Kirsty. "I wonder why?"

Kirsty followed her friend's gaze. Rachel was right. The other people out on the

slope looked mopey and bored. Nobody
seemed to be in a holiday mood at all!

"That's weird," Kirsty said, puzzled.
"The sun's shining, the sky's blue, and
the snow's perfect. What could be the
problem?"

"I don't know," Rachel said. "But I've
got a funny feeling something's not right."

It started to snow just then, and the air
was full of beautiful sparkling
snowflakes swirling in little
whirlwinds. Suddenly, Kirsty
noticed one extra-sparkly
snowflake that landed on
the branch of a nearby
tree. Curious, she went
for a closer look. There,
behind it, was Gabriella
the Snow Kingdom Fairy!

"Rachel!" Kirsty called. "Over here!"
She hurried to see what their new fairy
friend was doing back in the human
world.

"Hello, Gabriella!" Kirsty smiled. Then
her face fell as she realized that Gabriella
didn't look happy. "Is
everything all right?" she
asked as Rachel joined
her by the tree.

"It's Jack Frost again," Gabriella told
them. "This time he's stolen the magic
chest full of festive spirit!"

"Festive spirit?" Kirsty echoed. "What's that?"

"It's a magic potion," Gabriella explained. "It's kept inside a silver chest in the Fairyland palace. While it's there, it ensures that parties and special occasions are fun for all humans and fairies. Whenever there's a special event, like tomorrow's festival, I release the festive spirit from the chest, and the celebrations become even more wonderful."

Rachel remembered all the gloomy-looking people they'd seen that morning and something clicked in her mind. "Now that Jack Frost has the festive spirit, does that mean people won't be in a party mood?" she guessed.

"That's right," said Gabriella. "I was hoping to make the village festival really great tomorrow, but if no one feels happy, it'll be ruined!"

"How did Jack Frost manage to steal the potion?" Kirsty asked.

"He dressed up as a caroler," Gabriella explained. "Then he snuck into the Fairyland palace and stole the silver chest. He's taken it to his castle."

"We'll help you get it back," Rachel said at once.

An anxious expression crossed Gabriella's face. "That's very nice of you," she said, "but I'm afraid there's only one way we'll be able to do that." She swallowed and looked nervous. "We'll have to go into Jack Frost's castle ourselves!"

Outside the Ice Castle

Rachel and Kirsty felt a little frightened at the idea of going into Jack Frost's castle. They'd been there before with Holly the Christmas Fairy, and both girls knew what a cold, scary place it was.

"We've got to do it," Kirsty said after a moment. She did her best to sound brave and confident.

Rachel had a determined look in her eyes. "We managed it once, so we can do it again," she agreed. "We can't let Jack Frost ruin the festival!"

Gabriella smiled. "I was hoping you'd say that," she told them. "I'll take you to Fairyland right now!" She waved her wand and lots of snowball-shaped sparkles streamed around the girls. Kirsty and Rachel felt as if they were spinning

into a whirlwind. All they could see were blue and red stars. When the mist cleared, they were lowered to the ground again.

The three of them were standing near a holly bush covered in berries.

"We're fairies!" Kirsty cheered. She peeked over one shoulder to examine her delicate fairy wings. They shimmered in the winter sunshine. She couldn't resist giving them a gentle flutter so that she lifted off the ground. She loved being able to fly!

Rachel fluttered into the air, too — but as she rose up, she saw what was on the other side of the holly bush. Jack Frost's Ice Castle! Rachel gulped. In the excitement of

becoming a fairy, she'd almost forgotten
why they were here.

The castle was built from sheets of
gleaming ice and had four towers with
ice-blue turrets. The last time the girls
had been here, they had thought that
it looked lonely — today, however, it
seemed much livelier.

Rachel motioned to her friends. "Have

you seen what the goblins are doing?" she whispered.

Gabriella and Kirsty flew up to take a look. The castle was swarming with Jack Frost's goblins, who were working busily to prepare for the party. Some goblins were hanging icicle streamers, while others were blowing up ice-blue balloons.

One goblin stood on the highest tower, hanging up a large flag with Jack Frost's picture on it.

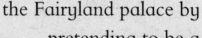

"We'll never be able to get into the castle with all those goblins around," Kirsty said in dismay.

Rachel remembered what Gabriella had said about Jack Frost sneaking into the Fairyland palace by pretending to be a caroler. "Maybe if we disguise ourselves, we'll be able to get past the goblins," she suggested. "How about if we're dressed as delivery people who have an urgent package for Jack Frost? That way they'll have to let us in!"

"Let's see if my fairy magic can make something special," Gabriella said as she waved her wand.

Glittering blue fairy dust danced in the air and a fabulous three-layer cake covered in thick, white frosting appeared. All around the outside of the cake, from top to bottom, ran a miniature twisty slide.

"Look who's on the slide!" Kirsty cried in excitement. "A tiny model of Jack Frost, on a candy sled!"

TO: JACK FROST,
ICE CASTLE,
FAIRYLAND.

"And here are the goblins!" Rachel laughed, pointing out the miniature green figures, who were throwing snowballs at one another, skiing, and sledding. Jack Frost's beloved snow geese rested on a silvery icing pond. The word "Celebrate" was written on the bottom layer in glitter.

"It's fantastic!" Rachel said, smiling at Gabriella.

"Thank you," Gabriella replied, blushing modestly. "Now I'd better give us all something to wear!"

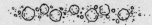

She waved her wand again and blue
sparkles tumbled around the three of
them. Kirsty and Rachel looked down at
themselves to see that they were now
wearing red delivery jumpsuits that

covered their wings, purple tops, and red baseball caps.

Gabriella was also in a delivery uniform. She quickly tucked her wand into the pocket of her jumpsuit.

"We're all ready," she said. "Let's go!"

A Very Special Delivery

Kirsty, Rachel, and Gabriella set off for
the castle with the cake. "Delivery!" they
called out as they approached the huge
double doors, which were guarded by a
pair of goblins. It was so cold, icicles
hung above their heads.

"Special delivery for a . . ." Rachel

pretended to be reading a label on the cake stand. "A Mr. Jack Frost!"

The goblin guards were very interested in the cake when they saw it. "Ooh, cake!" said one goblin with greedy eyes. "Can we eat it now?"

"I'm starving," the second goblin said, licking his lips. He tried to scoop up some of the icing with a warty finger, but Kirsty batted him away. "Excuse me," she said importantly. "I don't

think Mr. Frost will be very happy if his cake arrives all covered in goblin fingerprints!"

The goblin shrank back at her words. "Sorry," he muttered.

"Which way to the kitchen, please?" Rachel asked, taking a step closer to the doors. Her heart thumped and she crossed her fingers behind her back, willing the guards to let them in.

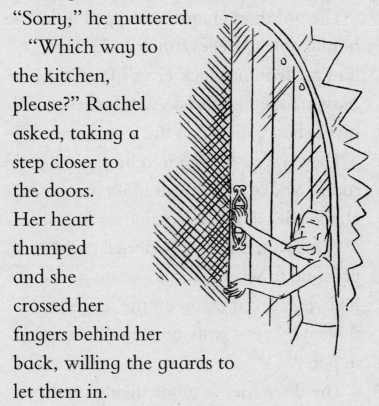

"Straight through the doors. Take the first hallway on your left, and follow it around," the greedy-eyed goblin said, pushing open the enormous metal doors.

The girls and Gabriella stepped inside, hardly able to believe their luck. They had made it into Jack Frost's Ice Castle! Now all they had to do was find the silver chest containing the festive spirit.

They were standing in a huge, chilly room. Above their heads hung a chandlelier made of ice diamonds.

"This way, I guess," Gabriella said, pointing to where a dark, gloomy hallway curved away on the left. She shivered. "Let's walk quickly. It's freezing in here!"

The three friends made their way down the hallway and found a large, brightly

lit kitchen at the end. A goblin chef with a tall white hat was blending silvery-blue ice cream when they entered.

"We're just delivering this," Kirsty told the chef, carefully setting the cake down on a table.

The chef barely looked up from his mixing bowl. "Thanks," he said, then stared at a recipe book. "Stir until ice crystals appear," he muttered to himself. "Um . . . I was just wondering," Rachel said. "I don't suppose you've seen a silver chest anywhere in the castle, have you?"

"Or a bottle of violet-colored liquid?" Gabriella added hopefully.

"What's this, twenty questions?" the goblin grumbled, as he stirred his mixture. "I don't have time for anything except party food right now, OK?"

"So you haven't seen the silver —" Kirsty began, but the goblin glared at her.

"I'm busy!" he snapped. "Now go away!"

Kirsty, Rachel, and Gabriella left the room quickly and huddled outside. "What now?" Rachel wondered. "This castle is huge. The festive spirit could be anywhere!"

Kirsty thought hard. Then an idea popped into her head. "Would you be able to turn yourself into a really tiny fairy, Gabriella?" she said, thinking out

loud. "Then you could hide in my pocket. Rachel and I could get ourselves captured by the guards, and —"

Rachel interrupted. "Captured?" she echoed.

"Yes," Kirsty replied. "If we're captured, the guards are sure to take us to Jack Frost. Then we can tell him we broke in to get the festive spirit, and . . ."

Rachel and Gabriella were both staring at Kirsty as if she were completely crazy, but she continued talking. "We can make Jack Frost believe that Gabriella is on her way back to Fairyland with the silver chest," she explained. "Jack Frost is sure to panic and rush to wherever he's keeping the festive spirit to see if it's still there. Then we'll find out where he's been hiding it!"

Rachel and Gabriella tried to take all of this in. "It's a clever idea," Rachel replied after a moment.

"But risky," Gabriella said. Her pretty face crinkled with doubt.

"Well, I can't think of any other way to find out where the festive spirit is hidden, can you?" Kirsty asked them.

Her friends shook their heads.

"That settles it, then," Kirsty said. "We'll have to try. Now, how should we get ourselves captured?"

Caught by the Guards!

"Wait," Gabriella said. "What will we do once we've found out where the festive spirit is? Try to grab it and fly off with it?"

Kirsty hesitated. "Um . . . I hadn't thought that far ahead," she confessed. "I'm not sure. I guess we'll just have to decide when we see it."

They all looked at one another.
Getting taken to Jack Frost with no
real escape plan seemed very dangerous.
But, as Kirsty said, they didn't have
any other ideas right now.

"Well, here
goes," Gabriella
said. She sprinkled
some blue and red
fairy dust over
herself. Immediately,
she began shrinking
until she was as small
as Kirsty's little finger.
"Will that do?" she asked,
her voice a tiny squeak.

"Perfect," Kirsty said, and pulled open
her pocket so Gabriella could slip inside.

Then she looked at Rachel. "Now to get ourselves captured!" she said, trying not to sound as nervous as she felt. Rachel nodded. "Let's go back to the big hall," she suggested. "We can pretend to be spying, and hope some of the goblins spot us."

Once they were in the icy hall, the two friends began prowling around, calling out to each other in loud, clear voices. "Well, she's not down

here," Kirsty bellowed, pretending to search behind a tall metal coat-stand.

"No, she's not over here either," Rachel shouted back, peering behind some midnight-blue curtains at one of the windows.

"I hope she gets away without Jack Frost catching her!" Kirsty called.

"Hey!" came a voice just then. "What's going on here?"

Two goblins had appeared. Rachel

and Kirsty pretended to gasp in fright. "Oh no!" Rachel cried.

"We've been caught!" Kirsty wailed.

"You certainly have," one of the goblins said, stalking toward them with an unpleasant smile. "Looking for something? Spying in the boss's castle?"

"Take them to the dungeon!" the second goblin declared. "Let's lock them up. Spies deserve nothing less."

Rachel and Kirsty exchanged glances. If they were locked in the dungeon, they'd have no chance of seeing Jack Frost! "As long as you don't take us to Jack Frost," Rachel begged desperately. "He's so scary!"

The goblins looked at one another. "On second thought," one of them said, "let's take them to Jack Frost. I wonder what he'll say when we tell him you've been spying?"

"Oh no," Kirsty cried. "We're going to be in so much trouble!"

The goblins looked pleased. "Yes, you are," they said, taking Kirsty and Rachel by their wrists. "This way!" The goblins hauled the girls along a stone hallway into the Great Hall. Jack

Frost sat the end of the room on a huge, icy throne. He looked up when he saw the girls enter with his guards. A suspicious gleam came into his eyes. "You two!" he said, recognizing Kirsty and Rachel, despite their delivery uniforms. "What are you doing here?"

"They were spying," one of the goblins said, pushing the girls roughly toward Jack Frost. "We caught them!"

"Spying, eh?" Jack Frost glared at Rachel and Kirsty. "I should have known. What did you hope to find?"

"Well . . ." Rachel said timidly, scuffing her foot along the ground. She hesitated, so it would seem like she didn't want to tell him anything.

"I'm waiting!" he snapped in an icy voice.

"We were trying to get the festive spirit back for the fairies," Kirsty said after a few moments.

"Of course," Jack Frost said. "Meddling again. How did you get here?"

"Our friend Gabriella the Snow Kingdom Fairy brought us to Fairyland," Rachel told him meekly.

"Did she? And where is she now?" Jack Frost asked, leaning forward on his throne.

Rachel and Kirsty exchanged glances. They didn't want to tell any lies about where Gabriella was, but at the same time they really wanted Jack Frost to think that she had already taken the festive spirit away. "I . . . I can't see her anywhere," Kirsty said truthfully. "Maybe she's gone back to the other fairies."

Jack Frost frowned and stroked his bony chin. "But if she came to get the festive spirit, why would she leave

without it?" he wondered. Then a thought struck him. "Unless . . ." He jumped off his throne with a gasp of horror. "Unless she's already got it!"

Kirsty and Rachel watched as Jack Frost rushed over to a pattern carved into the floor. It looked like a puzzle made from blocks of ice. What was he doing?

Jack Frost rearranged the squares of ice so that a picture of his face appeared on the blocks. When the picture was complete, he opened a trapdoor in the puzzle and took out a silver chest.

Kirsty held her breath. That had to be the Fairyland chest  containing the festive spirit! Jack Frost held up the chest with a grin. "Ha!" he gloated. "Your friend failed. I still have the festive spirit right here!"

Rachel swallowed nervously, and looked at Kirsty. What should they do now? She wished they'd thought out their

plan more carefully. The two goblin
guards were still in the room, and so
was Jack Frost. There was no way she
and Kirsty would be able to escape with
the chest!

Spread a Little Happiness

An idea came to Rachel just in time.
"Are you *sure* that's the real chest?" she
asked Jack Frost. "Someone might have
put a fake one in there just to trick you."

Jack Frost looked worried. "Do you
mean *you* put a fake chest in there?" he
demanded.

Rachel shrugged, trying as hard as she could to stay calm. It was difficult with Jack Frost staring right at her! "You won't know until you look, will you?" she asked.

Jack Frost kept looking from the girls to the chest, clearly debating what to do. Eventually, it seemed he couldn't handle not knowing . . . so he opened the chest.

Kirsty and Rachel watched anxiously
as Jack Frost lifted out a crystal bottle
with some violet-colored liquid inside.
The bottle had a glass stopper studded
with a glittering diamond. Jack Frost
pulled out the stopper and sniffed the
contents.

As he sniffed, the girls saw a sparkling
purple vapor swirl out of the bottle and
waft around Jack Frost's head.

He replaced the
stopper, and a
dreamy expression
spread over his
face. He smiled in
wonder at the
bottle, and put it
carefully back in
the chest.

Kirsty felt something wriggling in
her pocket and looked down. Gabriella
was peeking out, doing an excited
dance. "The festive spirit has put Jack
Frost in a really happy holiday
mood!" the tiny fairy whispered
breathlessly.

Jack Frost in a good mood? That didn't
happen very often! Kirsty seized the
opportunity to ask him a question. "I was
wondering," she said politely, "would it
be all right if we took the chest back to
the fairies now? It would be so great
to give everyone happy holidays with
the festive spirit."

Jack Frost seemed delighted by the
suggestion. "Of course! My pleasure,"
he said, closing the latch on the silver
chest and handing it to Kirsty.

"There's nothing I'd like more than to
see everyone enjoying the holidays."

"Thank you," Kirsty said. "That's
very kind. I hope you like your cake, by
the way!"

"Cake?" Jack Frost marveled. "For me?
Oh, this is the best day!"

"Let's go," Gabriella whispered,
"before the effects of the festive spirit
wear off!"

Rachel, Kirsty, and Gabriella left the throne room and made their way out of the castle very quickly. They didn't want Jack Frost to change his mind!

Outside, Gabriella did a delighted spin through the air. "Fantastic work, girls," she cried. "You were terrific in there!"

"Is there enough festive spirit left for the Winter Festival tomorrow?" Rachel wondered. "It seemed as if a lot came out when Jack Frost opened the bottle."

Gabriella smiled and magically grew back to her normal size. "Don't worry," she said. "The festive spirit replenishes itself overnight. There will be plenty more by tomorrow morning. The festival is sure to be a success." She patted the chest happily and tucked it under one arm. "Thanks again," she said. "The winter holidays have been saved, and it's all because of you. Everyone will be in a happy mood now that I have the festive spirit back. I'll send you to your world now, to enjoy the rest of the holidays — and the festival too, of course!"

"We will," Rachel assured her, waving to the fairy. "Thanks, Gabriella. Good-bye!"

"Good-bye!" Kirsty called, as Gabriella waved her wand over them again.

Everything blurred as they were whisked away by fairy magic. Seconds later, they were their normal size and back at the ski lodge in their ski outfits. They could hear whoops of laughter coming from the nearby slopes.

Kirsty grinned at the sound. "It seems like the festive spirit is working already," she said.

"Hooray for happy holidays!" Rachel cheered.

Quest for Fire

Contents

A Winter Chill

The next day, Kirsty and Rachel spent hours skiing and snowboarding on the slopes. Gabriella's festive spirit was working wonderfully — everyone was laughing, smiling, and really enjoying themselves.

"That was great," Rachel said happily, as they headed back to the ski lodge later that afternoon. "I'm looking forward to warming up in front of the fire now, though. I'm freezing!"

"Me, too," Kirsty said. "I love having a big roaring fire in the lodge every evening. It gets so cozy in there."

But when they went inside, both girls were surprised and disappointed to discover that there *was* no fire. Mr. Tate was crouching in front of the hearth, looking fed up. "I can't get it to light," he told the girls. "We've all tried, but the flame won't catch." Rachel shivered. "It's so

cold in here," she said.
Mrs. Walker hugged
her for warmth. "Don't
worry," she assured
her. "We'll just have
to head down to the
village earlier than
we'd planned. The
Winter Festival starts
soon, and there'll be
a big bonfire. We can warm up in front
of that."

"There are going to be fireworks later,
too," said Mrs. Tate. "And a craft fair
with people selling gifts."

"And best of all," Mr. Walker said,
pulling on his coat, "some stalls selling
hot food and drinks. What are we
waiting for?"

Kirsty and Rachel went to the coat room to put on their jackets, hats, and scarves again. As Rachel picked up her gloves, a burst of sparkles floated up from one of them . . . and out flew Gabriella!

"Oh, girls," she said urgently. "I need your help again — and fast! I've got to find the magic firestone as soon as possible!"

Kirsty glanced toward the main living room of the lodge where her parents were standing. "We can't let our parents see you," she whispered to Gabriella, motioning her and Rachel into a nearby closet. "What happened?" Kirsty asked.

"The magic firestone is kept in the hearth of the Grand Hall in the Fairyland palace," Gabriella explained. "It makes sure that humans and fairies can light fires for warmth and cooking. But Jack Frost was so angry about being tricked into giving back the festive spirit, he sent his goblins to steal the firestone and hide it in the human world. Now

that the firestone is missing, there can be no fire in the human world or in Fairyland. Jack Frost is determined to ruin the winter fun!"

"So that's why our parents couldn't light a fire here in the ski lodge," Kirsty realized.

"Yes," Gabriella said. "I'm sure the goblins with the firestone are somewhere at the festival in the village."

"We're going there with our families," Rachel said. "We'll help you search for goblins — and the firestone! What does it look like?"

"It looks likes an ordinary rock, but it's

surrounded by magical flames," Gabriella
said. "If you see any sort of flame, the
firestone is sure to be nearby."

Gabriella hid in the
folds of Rachel's scarf
and the two girls
slipped out of the closet.
"Ready when you are!"
Kirsty called to her parents.

The two families set off into the
village. It was dark now, but strings of
twinkling lights had been hung from the
branches of the trees to show the way.
At the festival, there were crowds of
adults and children bundled up in thick
winter coats and hats. They crowded
around the craft stalls that lined the
village street.

"Where's the bonfire?" Rachel wondered, trying to peer through the crowd.

"I heard it was going to be in the town square," Mr. Walker replied. "This way."

They squeezed through the stalls that

were selling festive gingerbread, painted wooden toys, furry mittens, and all sorts of other gifts. "Here's the square," Mr. Tate said, as they came out at the end of the street. "Oh dear," he added, as he saw the huge unlit bonfire in the center. "It seems like *they're* having trouble getting their fire started, too!"

Rachel and Kirsty stood and watched as a couple of men tried to light the enormous bonfire. "I can't even get a spark, let alone a flame from these matches," they heard one of the men grumble. "What are we going to do when it's time to set off the fireworks?"

Kirsty nudged Rachel. This was all because the magic firestone was missing! If they couldn't find the firestone in time, the bonfire and fireworks would never be lit — and the festival's finale would be ruined!

Green Elves

Mrs. Tate gave each of the girls some money. "Take a look around the stalls on your own, if you want," she told them. "Let's meet back here in an hour."

Rachel and Kirsty were excited. "Now we can look for the firestone," Rachel whispered after they'd said good-bye to their parents.

"Remember to watch out for any flames — and for goblins!" Gabriella reminded them, peeking out from behind Rachel's fluffy scarf.

"Let's wander around this side of the square," Kirsty suggested. "Look, there are some ice sculptures down here."

The friends headed for the ice statues Kirsty had spotted. A couple of sculptors were carving shapes from huge blocks of ice with silver chisels. There was an ice swan, an ice polar bear with an ice fish in its mouth, and even an ice rabbit, with its ears perked up.

"No sign of the firestone, though."
Gabriella sighed, gazing around. "Let's
look at the rest of the stalls."

The girls walked along, looking
carefully for any sign of flames. After a
while, they saw a stall that claimed to be
run by "Santa's Elves." There were a lot
of people gathered around the stall,
which was selling something called
"Toasted Bogmallows."

"Bogmallows?" Kirsty read in surprise. "What are they?" She and Rachel went closer to see. The bogmallows looked just like big green marshmallows.

Then Rachel noticed how green the "elves" running the stall were. "Goblins!" she hissed to her friends.

"And there's the firestone!" Gabriella added in an excited whisper. She pointed a finger to where a large glowing stone sat on the counter, surrounded by a magical flame. Above, piles of gooey green marshmallows toasted on a metal rack. Gabriella shook her head. "I can't believe they're using such a powerful stone to warm their silly bogmallows," she said. "I'm glad we know where it is, at least."

Rachel watched as people lined up, paid, and were told to help themselves to toasted bogmallows from the counter. "Is the firestone very hot?" she asked Gabriella in a low voice.

Gabriella shook her head. "It isn't hot to the touch," she replied. "It's heating the bogmallows with special fiery magic."

"Maybe Kirsty and I should each buy a bogmallow and try to grab it?" Rachel suggested.

"Good idea," Gabriella said.

Kirsty agreed. "Let's give it a try!"

An Ice Idea

Rachel and Kirsty joined the line for bogmallows. They pulled their hats low over their eyes and wound their scarves high around their faces, hoping the goblins wouldn't recognize them. The goblins were very busy, however. Some were opening new bags of bogmallows for toasting, others were counting out

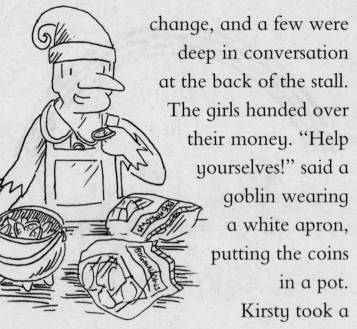

change, and a few were deep in conversation at the back of the stall. The girls handed over their money. "Help yourselves!" said a goblin wearing a white apron, putting the coins in a pot.

Kirsty took a bogmallow and stretched out her hand to grab the firestone. But just as her fingers were about to close around it, a goblin hand snatched the stone away.

Rachel took a bogmallow, too, and the girls moved to the side of the stall.

"Rats," Kirsty muttered. "I almost had it!"

"We'll have to think of another plan," Rachel said, nibbling her bogmallow. It was delicious — just like a toasted marshmallow.

The two girls and Gabriella all perked up their ears when they realized what the goblins were discussing.

"Jack Frost already has everything he needs," one of the goblins grumbled. "How are we supposed to think of a good present to give him at the party?"

"You know what he's like," a second goblin complained. "He'll be really angry if we don't find the perfect gift."

The goblin in the white apron, who'd been working at the front of the stall, turned to face the arguing goblins with his hands on his hips. "If you don't start helping sell these 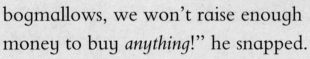 bogmallows, we won't raise enough money to buy *anything*!" he snapped.

"Hmmm," Rachel said. "Maybe if we offer the goblins a present for Jack Frost, they'll agree to exchange it for the firestone."

"Good idea," Kirsty said, "but what? It would have to be amazing to make them want to swap."

The three friends thought hard for a few moments. Then an idea popped into Rachel's head. "Gabriella, would you be able to create an ice statue like the ones we saw the sculptors working on earlier?"

"Of course," Gabriella replied. "But why?"

Rachel grinned. "I thought of the perfect present for Jack Frost," she explained. "An ice sculpture of himself! It would be a great centerpiece for his party!"

Kirsty's face lit up. "That's a terrific idea!" She laughed.

"We all know how vain Jack Frost is," Gabriella agreed. "He'll love it!"

Quickly, they all moved behind a booth so that no one could see them. Gabriella waved her wand and a large block of ice appeared. With a few sprinkles of fairy dust, a statue was created that looked just like Jack Frost. The ice

figure wore robes and a glittering crown.

"Wow," Rachel said. "That's fantastic!"

"It won't last forever, of course," Gabriella said, "even in Jack Frost's freezing castle. But it should last as long as the party does."

"That'll be fine," Kirsty said with a smile. "Now all we have to do is convince the goblins to exchange it for the firestone!"

Gift Wrapped

Gabriella sprinkled fairy dust on the
statue to make it lighter and easier to
carry, then returned to her hiding
place in Rachel's scarf. Kirsty and
Rachel lifted the frozen sculpture
and took it very carefully back to the
goblins' stall.

"We're all sold out," the goblin in the apron shouted to the others. He rattled the pot of coins. "What are we going to spend all this money on? Who's thought of a good present for Jack Frost?"

There was an uneasy silence as all the other goblins looked at one another and shuffled their feet.

"*We* thought of a good present!" Rachel called, as she and Kirsty carried the statue toward the booth. Gabriella leaned out from her hiding place and pointed her wand at the statue. With a bright blue flash of fairy magic, the

statue rose from the girls' hands and
floated over to the booth.

"Aarrrgh!" the goblins all screamed,
thinking it was their boss coming to
surprise them.

"It's a statue carved from ice," Kirsty said, trying not to giggle at the panicking goblins. "Isn't it good? We could make a trade — you give us the firestone, and you get this fabulous statue as a present for Jack Frost!"

The goblins looked relieved. "It does look like him," one of them said, leaning over the counter for a closer look. "But . . ."

"But what?" Rachel prompted.

"Well, it doesn't look much like a present, does it?" the goblin said, wrinkling his long nose.

"What do you mean?" Kirsty asked. "What *should* a present look like?"

The goblin shrugged. "Well, it should be wrapped up in paper, with a ribbon to untie, and . . ." Gabriella fluttered out from Rachel's scarf. "So if we gift wrap the statue, it'll be good enough?" she asked.

The goblins looked at one another. "Well, we don't have anything better, do we?" one of them muttered. That seemed to make up their minds. They turned back to the girls. "Yes," the goblin with the white apron said. "It's a deal — we'll trade it for the firestone, if you wrap up the statue nicely."

"OK," Gabriella said. She waved her

wand at the
statue, and fairy
dust flew all
around it.
Seconds later,
the statue was
covered in
holly-patterned
paper and tied
with a white
velvet ribbon.

"Yay!" cheered the
goblins, jumping up
and down.

"The fireworks will be starting in two
minutes!" a man with a megaphone
walked by and announced. "If we can
get them to light, that is," he added.

"Please make your way down to
the town square."

Rachel held out her hand for the
firestone. She had to get it back to
Gabriella before the fireworks
were ruined. "Firestone,
please," she said
to the goblins. But before
they could pass it to her,
a blast of freezing wind
blew in— and Jack
Frost himself
appeared!

Rachel and Kirsty ducked behind the booth before he saw them, and Gabriella darted behind the "Toasted Bogmallows" sign. Luckily, most of the people at the festival were making their way down to the town square, so no one had noticed the unusual arrival.

Jack Frost did not seem to be in a good mood. Kirsty held her breath as he stalked over to the goblins. She really didn't want him to spot her, Rachel, or Gabriella. He would be furious if he knew they were trying to get the firestone!

"The party's about to start," Jack Frost
said in an icy voice. "I want to know
where my present is!"

"It's here!" the goblins cried, rushing
out from behind the counter. "It's right
here. Open it!"

Jack Frost's gaze fell on the green present and his eyes glittered with excitement. He untied the ribbon and pulled off the wrapping paper.

Rachel and Kirsty anxiously watched as Jack Frost stared at the ice sculpture of himself. His spiky face didn't show any expression. He was speechless.

Rachel huddled closer to Kirsty, feeling

very tense. Both girls knew
what a terrible temper Jack
Frost had. If he didn't like
the gift, there was sure to
be trouble — and then
they would never get
the firestone back!

Fireworks!

"It's . . . it's . . ." Jack Frost stuttered.
Then he smiled. "It's fantastic!" He
walked all around the statue, looking at
every detail. "This is amazing. The
sculptor captured my star quality
perfectly."

The goblins grinned and high-fived one
another as Jack Frost struck a heroic pose

that looked just like
the statue.
"Wonderful," he
said happily. "The
best present ever!"

Kirsty nudged Rachel in
excitement. "He loves it!" she whispered.

Jack Frost clapped his hands. "Good
job, goblins!" he said. "I'll make sure

you all have a great
time at the party
tonight. I'll take
this back to
Fairyland
now. See you
later!" With
that, he vanished
in an icy
whirlwind.

Rachel and Kirsty came out from their hiding place. "A deal's a deal," Rachel said to the goblins, holding out her hand again. "Now can we please have the firestone?"

The goblins were almost jumping with joy. It was obvious that Jack Frost wasn't normally so nice to them.

"Here it is," the goblin in the white apron said, giving Rachel the firestone.

"Let's go to the party!" the other goblins cheered, and they all left. Rachel held the firestone out to Gabriella. The little fairy shank it with her wand so that she'd be able to take it back to Fairyland.

"Thanks again for all your help," the beaming fairy said, kissing both girls. "What would I do without you? Now I'd better bring the magic firestone to its rightful place in the Fairyland palace

hearth, so that the festival fireworks can
begin!"

"Bye, Gabriella," Kirsty said. "I really
enjoyed our adventures."

"Me, too," Rachel said. "Good-bye!"

Gabriella waved a hand and then flew
away. Soon she was only a bright blue
spark of light against the dark night sky.

"We'd better go find our parents," Kirsty said as they watched the fairy disappear.

The two girls walked toward the bonfire. Just as they reached the end of the street, a great cheer rose up from the town square. Rachel and Kirsty saw that the bonfire had finally been lit and bright flames were crackling all over the wood.

"Gabriella must have returned the firestone," Rachel said with a smile. "That was quick!"

"Just in time," Kirsty said happily, linking an arm through Rachel's. "Come on, let's hurry, before the fireworks begin!"

The two friends raced to join their parents and warm their hands by the blazing bonfire. Moments later, the first fireworks went off with pops and bangs. The sky was filled with beautiful colors and showers of bright sparks. The whole crowd *oohe*d and *ahh*ed in delight.

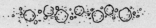

"I'm so glad we could help Gabriella the Snow Kingdom Fairy," Rachel said to Kirsty as they watched a firework explode in a flash of blue and red sparks.

Kirsty nodded. "Me, too," she said. "We've helped make the holidays wonderful for everyone!"

SPECIAL EDITION

Rachel and Kirsty helped Gabriella keep
the holidays festive, but Jack Frost is
causing even more trouble!

Can the girls save Christmas? Enjoy this
peek at

Holly

the Christmas Fairy!

A Magical Mistake

"Only three days to go!" Rachel Walker said, sighing happily. She was attaching Christmas cards to long pieces of red ribbon, so that she could hang them on the living room wall. "I love Christmas! Don't you, Kirsty?"

Kirsty Tate, Rachel's best friend, nodded. "Of course," she replied,

handing Rachel another pile of cards.
"It's a magical time of year!

   "Thanks for inviting me to visit," she
added, cutting another piece of ribbon.
"Mom says she and Dad will pick me up
on Christmas Eve."

   "We might get some snow before then!"
Rachel said, smiling. "The weather's
getting much colder. I wonder what
Christmas is like in Fairyland."

   When the girls had finished hanging
the Christmas cards, Rachel took Kirsty
out to the garage to find the boxes of
decorations.

   Rachel switched on the garage light.
"The decorations are up there." She
pointed at a shelf above the workbench.
"I'll stand on the stepladder and hand the
boxes down to you."

She climbed up the ladder and began to pass the boxes down. They were full of silver stars, shiny tinsel, and glittering balls in pink, purple, and silver.

"Oh!" Rachel gasped in surprise.

The gold locket around her neck had caught on a tiny, sparkling wreath made of twigs. The locket burst open, scattering both girls with fairy dust.

"What should we do?" Kirsty asked.

But they didn't have time to do anything. Suddenly, both girls were caught up in a swirling cloud of fairy dust that swept them off their feet. The sparkles whirled around them, glittering in the pale winter light.

"Kirsty, we're shrinking!" Rachel cried. "I think we're on our way to Fairyland!"

There's Magic in Every Series!

The Rainbow Fairies

The Weather Fairies

The Jewel Fairies

The Pet Fairies

The Fun Day Fairies

The Petal Fairies

The Dance Fairies

The Music Fairies

The Sports Fairies

The Party Fairies

The Ocean Fairies

Read them all!